Boodle

Boodle

Copyright © 2024 Verity James

All rights reserved.

The moral right of Verity James to be identified as the author of this work has been asserted in accordance with the Copyright, Designs and Patents act of 1988.

No part of this book may be used or reproduced in any manner whatsoever without written permission of the author or the publisher, except in the case of brief quotations embodied in critical articles or reviews.

This book is a work of fiction. Any resemblance to actual persons, living or dead, events or situations is purely coincidental.

Water colour paintings: Pauline Potterill

Editing & Formatting: Honesty Press

Published by www.honestypress.co.uk

ISBN: 978-1-739649593

First edition: April 2024

10 9 8 7 6 5 4 3 2 1

Boodle

Written by
Verity James

Watercolour paintings by
Pauline Potterill

Boodle meets Jamie.

Boodle meets Jamie.

Jamie walked along the country lane, keeping a sharp look-out for adventures. He had been looking for adventures all morning, but he had only seen two cows, a frog and lots of grass and trees.

"Perhaps I shall find an adventure round the next corner," he said to himself. But when he reached the next corner, all he could see were more trees and grass.

"Oh dear," he said sadly.

"Oh dear," said a small voice close beside him. Jamie was very startled and looked round to see who had spoken. Standing by the side of the road was a small furry animal with two very large and very sad eyes.

"What are you?" asked Jamie. "And what are you doing here?"

"I'm a boodle," answered the small creature. "And I'm standing here because I've nothing else to do. Who are you?"

"My name's Jamie and I'm looking for adventures," said the small boy. "What's your name?"

"My name's Boodle," said the boodle with a shy smile.

"Don't be stupid," said Jamie. "You can't be called Boodle if you're a boodle. Your name must be different from what you are.

I'm not called Boy, am I?" To his surprise, the boodle began to cry. The tears gathered in his big brown eyes and poured out on to his furry face.

"My name is Boodle," he cried. "It is, it is. All boodles are called Boodle. It's a well-known fact." And Jamie, who would not admit that he had never heard of this well-known fact, said quickly, "Of course, your name is Boodle. I'd just forgotten it for a moment." But the boodle would not stop crying.

"And I'm not stupid," he sobbed. "Boodles are not very clever, but they're not stupid. It's a well-known fact," he added tearfully.

"I didn't mean it," said Jamie, rather alarmed at this outburst. "I didn't really think you were stupid. I was just being cross." The tears stopped abruptly, and a big smile spread slowly across the boodle's face.

"Then I forgive you," he said generously. "And I'll help you look for adventures. What are Adventures?"

"Don't be stupid," said Jamie. "Everyone knows what adventures are." The tears welled up again and rolled down Boodle's face and on to his furry chest.

"Oh dear," said Jamie. "Do you have to keep crying like that?"

"All boodles cry when they're called stupid," said Boodle. "I don't like it because it makes my fur all soggy and it takes a long time to dry out. But I just can't help it," he sobbed.

"Oh dear," said Jamie. "I do wish you'd stop. I know you're not stupid," he added. The crying stopped immediately. Jamie gave his handkerchief to Boodle, who mopped up the tears vigorously.

"If you've finished crying, we could look for adventures together."

"Oh please," said Boodle. "I'm very good at looking for things because I have such big eyes. What does an Adventure look like?"

"It doesn't look like anything," said Jamie. "It's something that happens. Something exciting and dangerous. Or going to new places and meeting new people."

"Am I new?" asked Boodle.

"Yes," replied Jamie. "I've never met a boodle before."

"Then I'm an Adventure!" said Boodle, looking very pleased with himself.

"I suppose you are," said Jamie who hadn't thought of it in that way. Boodle's face went suddenly sad.

"Does that mean you don't want to look for Adventures, now that you've found one?"

"Oh, no," replied Jamie. "We can look for as many as we like." At this, Boodle beamed and together they walked along the lane.

Every now and then Boodle jumped into the air and sang, "boodly- boop-boop-de-boop." because he was feeling extra especially happy.

Boodle and the Sunglasses

Boodle and the Sunglasses

Jamie and Boodle were walking down the lane. It was a hot day and the sun was very bright.

"I think I'll have to wear my new sunglasses," said Jamie in a loud voice. He took them from his pocket and put them on, hoping that Boodle would notice and admire them. And, as all boodles are very observant, they were noticed immediately.

"Why are you wearing those?" asked Boodle.

"To keep the sun out of my eyes, of course," replied Jamie. "It's very bright today." "Yes, it is," said Boodle. He put his little furry paws over his eyes. "Oh, how bright it is! I can't see, it's so bright! Oh, it's hurting my eyes. I think I need some sunglasses to stop me from going blind in this bright sunshine."

"I'm sorry," said Jamie. "I've only got one pair and they wouldn't fit you. Your eyes are so much bigger than mine."

"They would fit me," said Boodle. "They look just the right size to me."

"Try them on then," said Jamie, and handed them over.

Boodle put them carefully on the end of his nose where they looked much too small.

"A perfect fit!" he declared and walked proudly along the road, holding his head well back so that the glasses would not fall off.

He walked straight into a tree and sat down with a bump. Jamie rushed up to him.

"Are you alright?" he asked. Boodle nodded sorrowfully.

"Maybe they were just a little bit too small," he said. "I had to cross my eyes to see through

them and I couldn't see where I was going." He began to cry.

"I need sunglasses," he sobbed. "All boodles need sunglasses. It's a well-known fact!"

Jamie took out his hankie and started to mop up the tears.

"Please don't cry, Boodle. I'm sure we can get a pair for you. We'll try the shop in the village, I bet they sell them in all sizes."

So, they went to the shop in the village which sold all sorts of glasses: plain ones, dark ones, and some with very fancy frames. They looked in the window but couldn't see any very large ones, so they went inside. A small, old man stood behind the counter.

"What can I do for you?" he asked.
"My friend, Boodle, would like some sunglasses. Extra large," said Jamie. "All boodles need sunglasses," explained Boodle.

"Indeed, indeed?" murmured the old man. "Then I shall have to see what I can do for you." He took several pairs of sunglasses from a case and tried them on Boodle. But they were all too small. Boodle was just beginning to look tearful again when the old man had an idea.

"Wait just a minute," he cried as he hurried out of the back of the shop. "I may have something to fit you." He came back with an enormous pair of dark glasses which he dusted well before handing to Boodle.

"These were part of a display, for advertising sunglasses. I was going to throw them away, but you might as well have them if they fit you." Boodle tried them on, and they fit perfectly.

"Thank you very much," he cried happily. Jamie thanked the old man too.

It was rather dark in the shop but Boodle refused to take off his new sunglasses, so Jamie had to lead him carefully into the street. Boodle stood on the pavement and looked about him.

"It's very dark," he said. "That's because the sun's gone in," replied Jamie.

Boodle peered over the top of his glasses.
"So it has," he said sadly. "Never mind," said Jamie. "You'll be able to wear them another day."

"That's true," said Boodle. A little more cheerfully. "That's very true."

Boodle and the Wimp and Wubberly Feeling

Boodle and the Wimp and Wubberly Feeling

Jamie walked along the lane looking for Boodle.

Something was wrong.

Usually, Boodle would rush along the lane to meet him shouting, "Hello, Jamie. Where are we going today, Jamie? Will we find adventures today, Jamie?" Then he would jump around a bit and squeak with excitement.

But today there wasn't a sound.

As he rounded a corner he saw Boodle sitting on the grass, looking very sorry for himself.

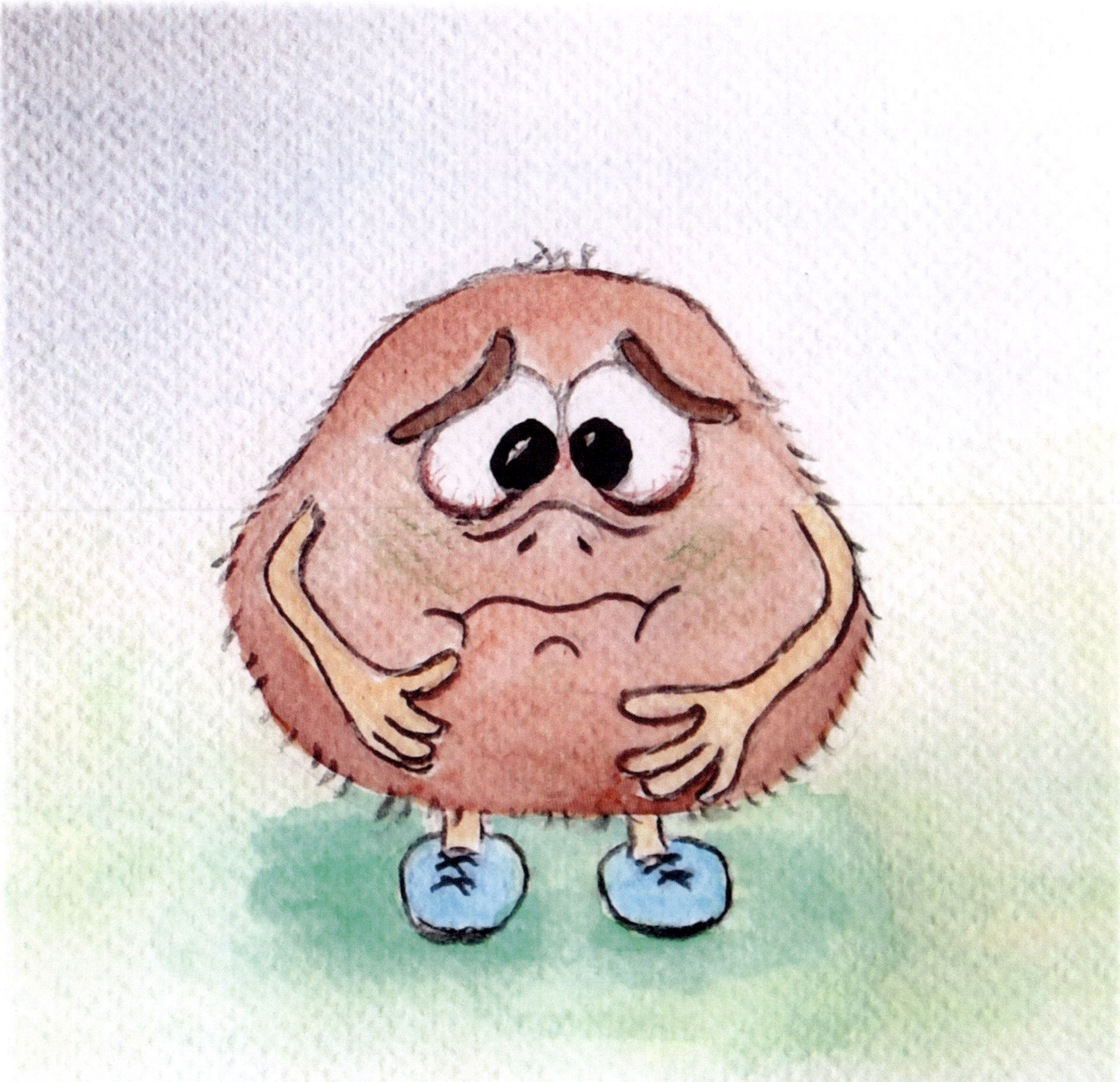

"What's the matter?" asked Jamie. Boodle clutched at his stomach and groaned.

"I've got a wimp and wubberly feeling," he said tearfully. "And it's a terrible feeling to have."

"I expect it is," said Jamie. "What does it feel like?"

"Sort of wimp at the edges and wubberly in the middle. Very wubberly in the middle," groaned Boodle.

"Is there anything I can do to help you?" asked Jamie, looking rather worried.

"I don't think so," said Boodle. "I shall just have to be very brave and bear this terrible pain."

"You really are being very brave," said Jamie.

"Yes, aren't I," said Boodle. "All boodles are very brave, you know. It's a well-known fact! What a pity this had to happen today when I had a surprise for you."

"I love surprises," said Jamie. "What is it?"

"It's something I found yesterday," said Boodle. "But it's a little way from here."

Although he was feeling very ill, he said he would be very brave and take Jamie to see the surprise. So, they walked along together, with Boodle groaning every now and then, just to remind Jamie how brave he was. They came to a tree and Boodle pointed to it proudly.

"There it is!" he cried.

Jamie looked at the tree. It was covered in small green apples.

"They're very small and rather sour," Boodle explained. "But there are lots and lots of them. If only I weren't feeling so wimp and wubberly, I could help you pick some." He groaned and sat down on the grass while Jamie gathered an armful of the apples.

They were sitting on the grass, eating the apples, when a car came along the lane. Jamie jumped up.

"It's the doctor," he shouted. "I'll ask him for some medicine for you."

"I only hope he's not too late!" cried Boodle. The doctor stopped the car and asked Boodle what the matter was.

"I feel wimp and wubberly," explained Boodle. "Especially in the middle. I feel very wubberly in the middle. Will you have to operate?"

"No," said the doctor. "But I'll give you some medicine." Boodle pulled a face, but he drank the medicine when Jamie reminded him how brave boodles were about taking medicine. "

What you're suffering from is a simple case of tummy-ache, and I suspect it was caused by eating too many little green apples," said the doctor.

"Oh dear," said Jamie and threw away the apple he was eating.

"That's not fair!" cried Boodle. "There ought to be a warning notice on the tree if the fruit makes you ill."

"Why don't we make one," said Jamie. "We could write a notice which says, BEWARE! THESE

APPLES WILL MAKE YOU FEEL WIMP AND WUBBERLY!"

"What a good idea!" said Boodle. "We'll do it tomorrow–... if you're feeling well enough."

Boodle and the Handkerchief

Boodle and the Handkerchief

Boodle and Jamie walked along the lane looking for beautiful stones. It was Boodle's idea. He had found a lovely smooth grey stone with white lines in it.

"Look!" he cried and held it out to Jamie. "It's just like a striped egg."

"That's nice," said Jamie, who thought that it looked just like a striped stone.

"Let's find some more," said Boodle, so they wandered along with their eyes on the ground. They found a lot more different shapes and colours, and soon they had their hands full of stones.

"We can't collect anymore," said Jamie. "They're getting too heavy to carry. And besides, most of these stones aren't even beautiful."

"They are," said Boodle tearfully. "All stones are beautiful. It's a well-known fact."

"No, it isn't," said Jamie crossly. "That's a stupid thing to say."

Huge tears poured from Boodle's eyes, ran down his check and plopped onto his furry chest.

"You shouldn't have said that," he cried in between sobs. "You know how boodles cry when they're called stupid."

"I'm sorry. I didn't mean it," said Jamie, though he was still feeling rather cross. He took out his handkerchief and mopped up Boodle's tears.

"And another thing," he said. "Why do you always have to borrow my hankie when you cry? Why haven't you got one of your own?" Boodle's eyes grew wide and sadder.

"How can I have a hankie?" he said in a very small voice. "When I haven't any pocket to put it in?"

Jamie suddenly felt very ashamed of himself for getting

cross. It was true. Boodles didn't wear clothes, so of course he had no pockets.

"Oh dear," he said. "I hadn't thought of that."

"It's quite alright," said Boodle generously. "You can't be expected to think of everything."

Jamie thought for a moment. "If we went to the shop in the village we could buy you a hankie," he said. "Then you could tie it on the end of a stick to carry over your shoulder. You could put things in it too, so it wouldn't matter about not having pockets."

"What a clever idea!" cried Boodle excitedly. "Let's do it straight away." So, they hurried to the shop, still carrying their stones, and stopping only to pick up a stick they found in a hedge.

The man in the shop spread his hankies all over the counter so that they could make their choice. Jamie liked the blue one best, but Boodle chose a large red one with white spots.

"I like it best because it's the brightest and biggest," he explained. They put the stones in the hankie and tied it by the corners to the stick. Boodle put it over his shoulder and strutted proudly out of the shop. After they had walked a little way, Boodle turned to Jamie.

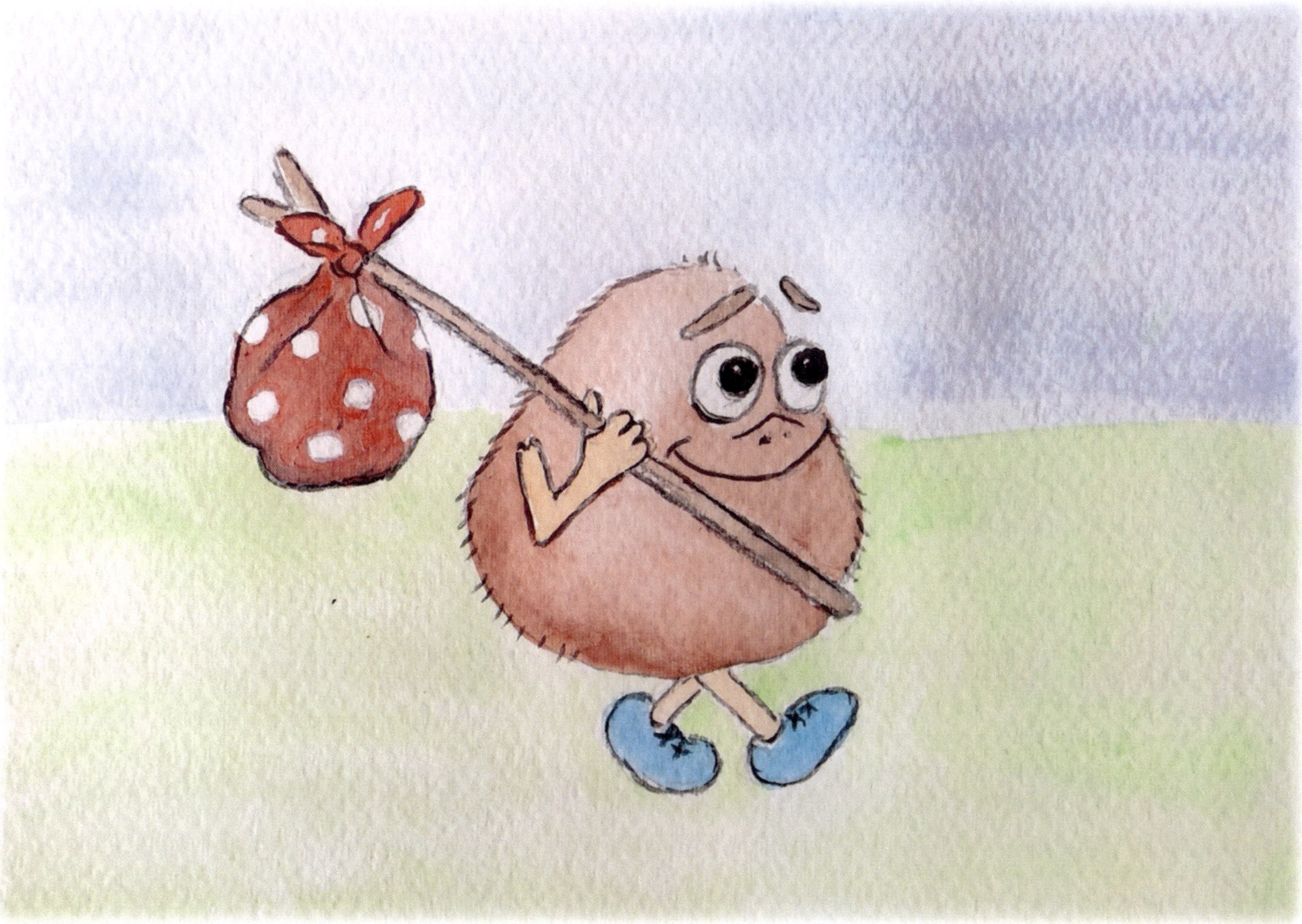

"As you are my friend Jamie, I'll let you carry my new hankie for a while, if you like," he said.

"Thank you," said Jamie, and put the stick with the hankie over his shoulder. After they had walked a little further Jamie said, "It's very heavy."

"Yes, it is rather heavy," said Boodle, "but you look very smart with it."

Fighting Dragons

Fighting Dragons

Boodle and Jamie were sitting in the sun, trying to decide what to do. "Let's go and fight dragons," said Jamie.

"Why?" asked Boodle.

"Because it would be exciting," said Jamie. "And dragons have to be killed."

"Why?" asked Boodle again.

"Because they are big monsters that eat people and breathe fire."

"Then isn't it rather dangerous to fight them?" asked Boodle.

"Of course," said Jamie. "That's what makes it exciting."
"Perhaps we won't find any dragons," said Boodle hopefully.

"Perhaps not," said Jamie. "There aren't many about."

"In that case, we'll go and look for one," said Boodle.

They looked for a long time, down the lane and through the fields, but found no dragons. It was very tiring to look for dragons on such a hot day, so they sat down to rest on the grass by an old stone wall.

Boodle saw a small creature lying on the wall. He nudged Jamie.

"Is that a dragon?" he whispered. Jamie looked carefully.

"I'm not sure," he said. "It looks like a dragon, but it's very small." Boodle turned to the animal.

"Are you a dragon?" he asked. The animal slowly opened one eye and stared at him.

"I'm a lizard," he said, with great dignity.

"What are you doing?" asked Boodle.

"I'm sitting in the sun," said the lizard. He sighed contentedly. "I really can't think of anything nicer to do than sit in the sun.

It's so warm and comfortable.
Why don't you try it?"

"I think I will," said Boodle. He lay back in the grass and closed his eyes. "You're right," he said. "It's very comfortable. Ve-ry com-fortable." He gave a sigh and was soon snoring gently.

"Are you sure you're not a dragon?" asked Jamie. "You're the right shape for a dragon, even though you are so small."

"I don't think I'm a dragon," said the lizard. "But I'm not full grown yet. Perhaps I'll be a dragon when I'm older. What are dragons like?"

"Oh, they're huge," said Jamie waving his arms about excitedly. "And they roar and breathe fire and eat people."

"Do they really?" asked the lizard. "What fun!"

"Why don't you try it?" said Jamie. "Go on – see if you can make a fierce roar." The lizard pulled a frightening face and tried to roar. All that came out was a tiny squeak.

"That wasn't very good," said Jamie.

"I tried my best," said the lizard crossly. "It's not my fault I'm not full grown. I bet I'll do better when I'm older."

"I'm sure you will," said Jamie. "Now try breathing out fire – just a spark will do." The lizard huffed and puffed as hard as he could, but he couldn't even make a spark.

"This is all very hard work," said the lizard crossly. "Does it really matter whether I'm a dragon or not?"

"Well, I did so want to meet a dragon," said Jamie.

"Why?" asked the lizard.

"So that I could fight it, of course," said Jamie.

"That's not very nice," said the lizard. "I thought you were my friend."

"I am," said Jamie. "I wouldn't fight you, of course – only big fierce dragons." The lizard looked at Jamie out of one eye.

"Does your friend fight dragons too?" he asked.

"He's not very keen on it," said Jamie. "He prefers to doze in the sun."

"How very sensible he is," said the lizard. "Why don't you try it? There's nothing quite so enjoyable as sitting in the sun."

So, Jamie sat on the grass and leaned against the wall. He

closed his eyes and enjoyed the feel of the warm sun on his face.

When the sun finally went behind some clouds, Jamie woke up Boodle and they said goodbye to the lizard.

As they were walking back across the fields, Jamie turned to Boodle and said, "I don't think I'll fight dragons after all. They're much too nice."

"I agree," said Boodle. "And besides, it's such hard work."

Honesty Press

Established 2022

WWW.HONESTYPRESS.CO.UK

Supporting very talented local, independent, and self-published authors.

Thank you for supporting us.

All our books are available at

www.honesty-press.sumupstore.com

Printed in Great Britain
by Amazon